# Auntie N[...] Magical Pockets

## Easy and Fun Ways to Help Children Cope with Everyday Stress

Monica H. Schaeffer, Ph.D., & Shelley R. Baker

illustrated by Janie Secatore

ISBN-10: 1490307877
ISBN-13: 9781490307879
Library of Congress Control Number: 2013909940
CreateSpace Independent Publishing Platform
North Charleston, South Carolina

## To Our Moms...

*Lilo Schaeffer* and *Sunny Tuck*, our biggest champions! Their love, support, and encouragement gave us the impetus to help children of all ages by bringing this storybook to light. Also to our children and grandchildren, who have and will continue to benefit from *Auntie Nellie's Magical Pockets* by using these practical tips to cope with everyday stressors.

## With Gratitude...

Auntie Nellie and Casey exist within these pages because of the contributions of a number of people whom we acknowledge with thanks.

To **Janie Secatore**, our illustrator, who brings to life not only our amusing, caring, and hip Auntie Nellie and our adorable, persevering Casey but all of Auntie Nellie's anti-stress gadgets. Always patient with us, Janie revised the illustrations many times, with no complaints but rather with a contagious energy and a twinkle in her eye.

To **Wendy Reiter, Carol Brody, Hilary Razon, Hillary Brooks, Joanna Walsh, Aimee Stone,** and **Dr. Barbara Brynelson**, our readers and reviewers, who include elementary school counselors, media specialists, therapists, pediatricians, and parents. Their encouragement and attention to detail are what make this storybook fun for children and helpful to parents and educators alike.

To **Joanne Brodsky**, our editor, whose keen eye caught our mistakes and made this finished book our pride and joy.

To **our families**, who gave us the inspiration to write this book in the first place, and who hopefully will use this book to fortify future generations with coping techniques for healthier tomorrows.

# Casey's Week

# With Auntie Nellie

# A NOTE TO PARENTS AND TEACHERS

This book has been written for children to provide them with easy and fun ways to cope with or handle everyday stress. We chose a storybook format that will entertain children while helping them learn important life skills and increase their repertoire of effective coping techniques.

In each chapter, our main character, Casey, tells a story about a common childhood situation that has caused him stress. He recounts his tales, and each time he explains how his Auntie Nellie helped him learn a new anti-stress technique.

Rather than focusing on ways to relieve stress, as does most of the current literature, our approach is preventive in nature. Our goal is to help children as young as four years old learn how to cope with a situation before it becomes stressful. The techniques we have chosen provide children with the ability to look at potentially stressful situations and react in a positive way. Research has shown that capable, well-adjusted adults who use these same techniques show more resistance to the harmful effects of stress.

All children will be able to relate to Casey, because they have been, or will soon find themselves, in many of the same situations. We have selected these situations after interviewing children and researching the literature to identify events considered to be stressful for children from four to seven years old.

We have included *Parent/Teacher Notes* (P/T Notes) for each chapter to provide you with a quick, helpful guide to the book. To be effective, you should read the P/T Notes for each chapter *before* reading the chapter to the child. The notes included in each chapter begin with a quote (labeled the **cue**) from Casey that summons Auntie Nellie's help. You are then provided with succinct explanations about both the **stressor** (the problem being faced by Casey) and the **technique** being offered by Auntie Nellie. Additional situations for which you may find the technique useful are also provided in the P/T Notes for Chapters 2-7. In most cases, situations can best be handled by selecting a combination of coping techniques. The last chapter, Chapter 8, illustrates this point.

Keep in mind that coping is not a static act but rather a dynamic process. When put in a potentially threatening situation, the more coping techniques a child can call upon or choose from, the more capable he or she will be in finding a remedy. Increasing a child's repertoire of effective coping techniques is the critical goal of this book.

After the child has read *Auntie Nellie's Magical Pockets*, you may want to play a game with the child to determine how much information has been comprehended and to reinforce the usefulness of the new coping skills. The child could be asked to describe what he or she would do if presented with certain situations or which of Auntie Nellie's gadgets he or she would use. The situations may be drawn from those listed in the P/T Notes section of each chapter. The anti-stress gadgets described in each chapter may be used as prompts or cues to remind the child of the various techniques that he or she can call upon. Giving the child ample opportunity to practice or rehearse these new coping skills is critical to building the child's confidence and ensuring his or her ability to call upon them when needed.

Just as reaching for and using a seatbelt becomes an automatic response for children before a car starts moving, thinking of Auntie Nellie's gadgets can also become automatic cues for using these anti-stress techniques. These new coping skills will contribute to improving their health not only for today, but for all their tomorrows to come.

Monica H. Schaeffer, Ph.D., and Shelley R. Baker

# CHAPTER 1

# My Auntie Nellie

Hello! My name is Casey. I live with my mom, dad, and baby sister, Ginger. I like playing games, going to school, and riding my bike. My favorite color is blue. My favorite food is pizza.

I love my Auntie Nellie, and I especially like when she visits us! She is so funny and makes me feel good. Before she came to visit, I used to get angry a lot, and sometimes I'd feel sad, scared, or just confused.

I also used to have lots of stomachaches and headaches, and I could never fall asleep at night. Auntie Nellie showed me lots of new ways to deal with things, and now I feel so much better.

What I like most about Auntie Nellie is her pockets! They are amazing and magical! She reaches down deep into them to pull out gadgets that help me with all sorts of situations.

Let me tell you about the week Auntie Nellie came to our house for a visit. That was the week my Auntie Nellie came to the rescue! I'll bet some of the things I learned from Auntie Nellie can help you, too.

# PARENT/TEACHER NOTES
## Chapter 1: Defining Stress

**Cue:** "I used to have lots of stomachaches and headaches, and I could never fall asleep at night."

**Problem:** Research has shown that there are a number of telltale signs of stress that children may exhibit. These often include the ones that Casey has described—stomachaches or queasy feelings, headaches, and trouble falling asleep. Others include excessive crying or whining, irritability, listlessness, irrational anger, poor eating, and frequent negative self-statements. Although all children exhibit these signs from time to time, it is important to identify any unusual and persistent deviations from their regular behavior.

All of these signs are what can be considered the stress reaction or response to a situation. To understand stress in children, you need to be able to view stress as a *3-step process*:

1. Events called stressors or sources of stress
2. The child's appraisal or perception of the event(s)
3. The child's resulting physical and psychological stress responses or reactions

In everyone, children and adults alike, the stress process begins when a person first evaluates a stressor's danger or threat potential. The body gets itself ready to combat the stressor (e.g., the heart beats faster, breathing quickens, palms feel sweaty, certain muscles contract). A coping technique is then put into action to help the individual adapt to the stressor. The effects of stress diminish if the coping technique is effective—the heart stops racing, breathing slows, and blood pressure decreases.

If an individual can't seem to handle the stressor, the stress reaction persists and the detrimental effects of stress become more likely. After repeated exposure to threatening situations, a child may come to believe that things are hopeless, and as a result, believe he or she is helpless or powerless. This is why it is vital to begin prevention early. Depression, suicide, and the use of drugs and alcohol are associated with chronic or long-term exposure to unmitigated stressors.

Auntie Nellie's mission is to help children take positive action to avoid becoming stressed out. In children, the stress reactions (the third component of the process outlined above) are probably the easiest part of the process to recognize. But the adult must pay attention to how a child perceives a threat, and how he or she copes with and adapts to it, as these are critical elements in learning to reduce the harmful physical and emotional effects of stress.

**Technique:** Throughout this book, Auntie Nellie describes coping techniques that children can easily use by themselves to diminish the harmful effects of stress. A key factor in all of these techniques is viewing stress as a process: the potential stressor is identified, the child's perception of the event is dealt with and put in a positive light, and the coping techniques selected prevent the stress reaction from persisting.

The book deals with six potential stressors for children who range in age from four to seven years old: getting ready by oneself (Chapter 2), learning something new (Chapter 3), getting teased by other children (Chapter 4), feeling ignored by busy parents (Chapter 5), handling a major disappointment (Chapter 6), and trouble falling asleep (Chapter 7). Chapter 8 illustrates how a combination of these techniques can be used effectively in other situations. Just as acquiring any new skill takes practice, adults should recognize that children will require time to practice these new coping skills in order to maximize their effectiveness.

In helping the child, you should first discuss the events that he or she is anxious, scared, or worried about and the reason why the events are being perceived as *threatening*. If the child mentions any of the situations described in this book, you can pique the child's interest by saying, "Let's find out what Casey did to help himself." You should contrast all of the stressors the child identifies as threatening with events or situations that he or she views as *challenging* rather than *threatening*. Although the child probably experiences similar physical reactions to challenges (e.g., heart racing, quicker breathing), they will not be accompanied by the negative feelings or thoughts associated with threats. Getting children to view and label potential stressors as *challenges* and not *threats* is critical to preventing the harmful effects of stress.

# CHAPTER 2

# YES, I CAN! YES, I CAN!

On school mornings, my house is a very busy place. My mom and dad need to get ready for work. They also have to feed my baby sister Ginger and get her ready for the babysitter. I help too by dressing myself, brushing my teeth, and tying my sneakers.

Some days I can do all of these things one-two-three. And then on other days, boy, do I have trouble! One morning during Auntie Nellie's visit, I was in the bathroom screaming, "Get on to the brush!" but the toothpaste wouldn't listen to me.

I shouted, "I CAN'T DO THIS!" as the toothpaste missed the toothbrush.

From around the corner, I heard a tiny voice that sounded just like mine say, "Yes, I Can! Yes, I Can!"

I looked around and whispered, "Who is that? That *can't* be me."

Just then Auntie Nellie popped into the doorway and asked, "Did I hear someone say, 'I can't do this?'"

"That was me, Auntie Nellie," I answered. "I can't do anything this morning. I can't button my shirt. I can't tie my sneakers.

And I can't get this toothpaste to stay on my brush!"

Just then I heard that same little voice that sounded just like mine.

"Yes, I Can! Yes, I Can!"

"Who said that, Auntie Nellie?"

Auntie Nellie reached way down into her magical pocket and pulled out a doll.

"Look, that's me!" I said. I was really excited. "But look, his shirt is buttoned, and his sneakers are tied!"

"That's right, Casey. This doll is a reminder that you *can* do these things—you have done them many times before," she said.

In her calm, soothing voice she continued, "You just have to keep telling yourself that you *can!* Now how about trying again? Only this time instead of saying 'I can't,' repeat Yes, I Can! Yes, I Can!"

So I tried to button my shirt while saying, Yes, I Can! Yes, I Can! and I did it all by myself! I didn't miss any holes.

"WOW," I said, "maybe this will help me tie my sneakers."

As I worked on making the bows, I whispered, "Yes, I Can! Yes, I Can!" and I heard the doll say, "Yes, I Can! Yes, I Can!"

"I did it! I did it! It worked again," I said with pride, showing Auntie Nellie two perfect bows.

"You see," said Auntie Nellie, "you did it just by believing in yourself. Instead of saying 'can't,' you said 'can.' By saying 'yes, I can,' you will be able to do lots of things, like pour milk into your glass without spilling it or zip up your jacket.

"Now, don't forget," she said as she pointed to the toothpaste.

"OK" I said. "Yes, I Can!" And I had the mintiest breath at school all day—at least until lunchtime.

# PARENT/TEACHER NOTES
## Chapter 2: Getting Ready by Oneself

**Cue:** "I can't do this!"

**Problem/Stressor:** Casey is extremely frustrated because he can't seem to perform certain tasks that he has completed successfully on other occasions. This problem or stressor is different from the one that is presented in Chapter 3 when Casey is learning something *new* and does not as yet possess all the skills to accomplish what he wants. In this chapter, Casey is overwhelmed and gives up trying all three tasks.

**Technique:** Auntie Nellie helps Casey by first reminding him that he has tied his sneakers, buttoned his shirt, and brushed his teeth many times before. Pointing this out to Casey helps him realize that in fact he *can* do all of these things; it's just today that he is experiencing difficulty. In this way, Auntie Nellie has reinterpreted the situation, making it much less threatening for Casey. Casey may have experienced difficulties for many reasons that are unrelated to his capabilities. They may include getting up late and being rushed or not getting enough sleep and, as a result, feeling tired.

Adults can help children reinterpret stressful situations and see the distinction between their capabilities and extenuating circumstances. Auntie Nellie uses the Casey doll to turn Casey's negative statements about himself into a very powerful, positive one: Yes, I Can. This technique is known as "cognitive restructuring" or simply turning one's negative thoughts and statements into more positive ones. Research has shown that simply thinking positive thoughts rather than negative ones can help people feel better and more relaxed.

Auntie Nellie then asks Casey to rehearse this new positive statement while he buttons his shirt. He then goes on to use it while he ties his laces and brushes his teeth. Auntie Nellie reminds him of other situations in which the statement may come in handy, such as pouring milk into a glass or zipping up his jacket. Cognitive restructuring works because it helps a child reinterpret the situation in much less threatening ways.

You may suggest more individualized examples of situations in which the child has experienced difficulties; *however, do not use examples of situations in which the child experienced difficulties as a result of not possessing or not having learned the skills necessary to complete the task.*

A key to using this technique successfully is to have the child approach the task or situation with a positive attitude. If you hear the child say, "I'm not very good at…" or "I can't…," show him or her that there are positive ways to talk to oneself. Encourage them to instead say things such as, "I'm working on it so I will be good at it," or "I've been able to do it before, so I'll be able to do it again. I just have to go a little slower this time." In certain cases in which the child is experiencing a lot of anxiety, you may want to write down all of the child's negative statements, and then take each one at a time and show him or her how a positive statement may be substituted. Having the child repeat each of the positive statements, as well as role-play the situation, can be a helpful addition to this exercise. An older child could, in fact, be asked to come up with his or her own suggestions for turning negative statements into positive ones.

**Other situations in which this technique may be helpful:**

- Going back to school after a long illness or a school vacation
- Putting together a puzzle
- Being scared about going to the dentist or doctor

# CHAPTER 3

# COUNT TO 10 AND TRY AGAIN

Every Tuesday, my class goes to the gym. We exercise, run races, and learn to use all different types of equipment. One day the teacher was showing us how to walk on the balance beam.

It was my turn and the teacher was saying, "Remember, Casey, arms out straight and toes pointed forward."

Oops! After taking just two steps, I lost my balance and landed on the mat with a thud.

"This is too hard!" I said, feeling miserable. I went off to sit in a corner and watch the rest of the kids. It looked so easy for everyone else.

Right at that moment, Auntie Nellie appeared in front of me, like magic. She had brought my lunch bag to school (I forgot it on the kitchen table).

"Are you hurt, Casey?" she asked me sweetly. "No scrapes or bruises that I can see," said Auntie Nellie after inspecting me from head to toe.

"No," I yelled, "but you won't find me trying to walk on that beam again." And then I started to cry. "Why can't I learn to do it like the other kids?"

While I was crying, I heard a funny noise. *Tick, Tick, Tick.* I asked Auntie Nellie, "What's that noise coming from your pocket?"

Auntie Nellie reached so far down into her pocket that her whole arm seemed to disappear. She then pulled out a funny-looking gadget! It was a giant ring that had little numbered doors all around it. The words, "Count to 10 and Try Again" were printed on the ring. It sounded like a clock. *Tick, Tick, Tick.*

"What is that, Auntie Nellie?" I asked. I wasn't crying anymore.

"It's a number counter. With each door you shut, you count from 1 to 10," Auntie Nellie explained.

"How can counting to 10 help me learn to walk the balance beam?" I asked.

Auntie Nellie told me, "Often when you are trying to learn something new, it's easy to get frustrated or upset if you can't do it right away. But it is important that you are willing to give it a few tries. That's what learning is all about."

She continued explaining this to me. "It helps stop the frustration if you take a break from what you are doing for just a short time. Counting to 10 helps clear your mind and calm you down. You can then think clearly about how you will try again."

"Now, let's try using the ring, Casey," said Auntie Nellie. "Count to 10 and Try Again."

As I shut each door, I counted. "1—2—3—4—5—6—7—8 —9—10." As I counted, I felt my body becoming less tense.

"Now take a deep breath through your nose, hold it, and let it out through your mouth," she continued. "Now you are ready to try walking on the balance beam again."

I was not too sure about this, but I ran back in line to try the balance beam again. This time my gym teacher said, "Much better, Casey. You have your arms in the right position, now just work on your feet!"

I ran back to Auntie Nellie saying, "Auntie Nellie, I got my arms right, but I couldn't get my feet."

"Wow, Casey, you almost did it! Now before you get upset about your feet, why not try the counter again. With most things, it takes a few tries."

I started shutting the doors and counting. "1— 2—3—4— 5—6 —7— 8—9—10." Then I took a deep breath through my nose, let it out through my mouth, and thought about pointing my toes straight ahead.

Then I tried again. This time I did it! My whole gym class cheered, "Hurray!" And I felt great!

# PARENT/TEACHER NOTES
## Chapter 3: Learning Something New

**Cue:** "This is too hard for me."

**Problem/Stressor:** Casey is in the process of *learning* a new skill on the balance beam. Learning new things can be very frustrating, especially if the child perceives that he or she should be able to do it on the first attempt and that it "looks so easy" for everyone else.

**Technique:** Auntie Nellie helps Casey by using a technique that combines distraction and relaxation. Such a technique is effective in breaking a negative cycle from recurring over and over again. The counter serves to distract Casey from thinking about the balance beam. The principle is that Casey can't count to 10 and be frustrated at the same time. By counting to 10, Casey is forced to take his mind off the balance beam for a short time. This allows Casey to clear his mind before trying again. After counting to 10, Auntie Nellie also tells Casey to take a deep breath through his nose, hold it, and let it out through his mouth.

Depending on the child's frustration level, this step may need to be repeated several times. The technique helps the body to relax. After counting to 10 and taking a deep cleansing breath, both the body and mind are ready to calmly confront the situation again. After counting to 10, taking a deep breath, and letting it out, Casey is able to concentrate on the aspect of the new skill giving him problems.

Auntie Nellie also makes the important point that learning something new often takes a few tries. Children may be eager to try something new, yet become easily discouraged and frustrated after a few unsuccessful attempts. You can help ease these feelings by gently reminding them of other accomplishments that the child achieved only after several attempts, such as hitting a baseball or riding a two-wheeled bicycle. Allowing the child to take short breaks or rest periods while learning something new is a good technique that incorporates the distraction and relaxation principles.

**Other situations in which this technique may be useful:**

- Learning to read
- Learning to ride a bike
- Learning a new sport

# CHAPTER 4

# WHO CAN I TELL?

On Thursdays I play T-ball after school and take bus #428 home. By the time I get home, it's almost time to eat dinner.

On the Thursday that Auntie Nellie was visiting, I couldn't think about dinner at all. I couldn't think about anything but what a terrible day I had.

I was in the kitchen when Mom announced, "We're having a barbecue for dinner, Casey. Do you want a hamburger or a hot dog?"

"I'm not hungry, Mom," I said.

"Why not?" she asked. "You're usually starving on Thursdays."

I wasn't really sure why I wasn't hungry. "I don't know," I answered, a little bit upset.

"Don't you feel well?" Mom asked with concern. She felt my head to see if I had a temperature.

"My stomach hurts," I said, but it wasn't the kind of feeling I get when I'm hungry.

"Maybe we should call the doctor," Mom said.

That did it. I burst into tears, and I couldn't stop crying. Mom ran over and gave me a hug that made me feel a little better. But I still had a stomachache and still felt like crying.

That's when Auntie Nellie took my hand and said "You'll feel a lot better, Casey, if you tell us what is really on your mind. What happened today?"

"I don't know," I cried.

My Auntie Nellie then reached really, really deep into her pocket and pulled out a bright blue megaphone with "Who Can I Tell?" written on it.

I couldn't believe she could fit that in her pocket! It was gigantic! "What's that for?" I asked her.

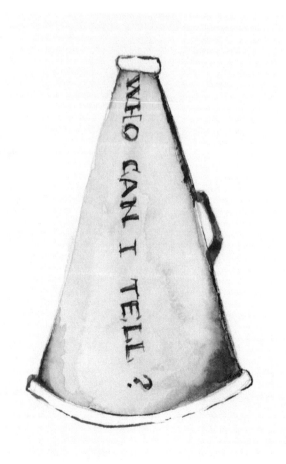

Auntie Nellie then put the megaphone up to her mouth, and her words came out loud and clear. "THIS MEGAPHONE IS TO REMIND YOU TO TALK, CASEY. TO TELL SOMEONE— ANYONE CLOSE TO YOU—WHAT IS ON YOUR MIND. ONCE YOU DO, YOU WILL FEEL MUCH, MUCH BETTER."

Through my tears, I let it out that some kids had called me stupid and teased me at school.

Auntie Nellie explained that just because the kids said it, didn't mean it was true. "Do they tease other kids?" Auntie Nellie asked.

I thought about it and remembered that they had teased my friend Tessa.

"Does anyone else tease you?" Auntie Nellie asked.

"Not really," I said. "Not like these kids do." I thought about it for a little more and realized that there were a lot more kids that liked me and never were mean to me.

"Thanks, Auntie Nellie," I said, giving her a hug. "It really helped for me to talk about this out loud with you. I feel much better now."

"As you get older, there will be times when your feelings will be hurt and you're not sure what to do," she said. Auntie Nellie then picked up the megaphone and shouted, "THE FIRST STEP IN HELPING YOURSELF IS TO LOOK AROUND AND THINK, *WHO CAN I TELL?*"

"Many times your teacher, parents, aunt, or good friend can show you that you are not alone in how you feel. Sometimes just talking about your feelings out loud and not keeping them inside can help you feel better."

My stomach started grumbling. I grinned and took the megaphone from Auntie Nellie, announcing, "I'M HUNGRY. LET'S EAT!"

# PARENT/TEACHER NOTES
## Chapter 4: Getting Teased by Other Children

**Cue:** "I don't want to talk about it" and "I don't know."

**Problem/Stressor:** Casey has been teased and called stupid by children at school. His lack of appetite and sudden outburst of tears are signs that he is under stress. Casey's responses of "I don't know" and "I don't want to talk about it" should not be ignored, but rather viewed as calls for help and understanding.

**Technique:** Auntie Nellie helps Casey by initially sensing that Casey is keeping something to himself when he suddenly bursts into tears after his mother's remark about calling the doctor. If a child is unusually whiny or cries easily at things that normally elicit a different response, you may want to ask the child, as Auntie Nellie asked Casey, "What really happened to you today?" Although for most children this question will provide a release for all of the feelings pent up inside, other children may need further prodding or encouragement to open up. Giving the child a warm hug *while* you ask questions can make a child feel more secure to discuss his or her feelings.

With her "Who Can I Tell?" megaphone, Auntie Nellie is teaching Casey to understand the power of his own voice through verbalizing his feelings, as well as the importance of using his social support network. Social support or the knowledge that one is cared about and valued by others has been shown to be a powerful mediator of stress.

Auntie Nellie helps Casey by reminding him that, even though children have called him stupid, it doesn't mean that it is true. This social support helps Casey, because it allows him to gain a variety of perspectives or interpretations of the situation. In addition, talking through problems with others who care reinforces the child's value. The support can then be called upon in future situations as a kind of protection or armor.

**Other situations in which this technique may be useful:**

- Feeling left out of social situations
- Getting in trouble at school
- Getting a bad grade in school

*Author's Note: If you think a child is being bullied, you should consult your school system for information on the specific procedures that have been adopted for dealing with this serious issue.*

# CHAPTER 5

# SUPER C

I used to hate weekends. Weekends were always the same. Dad was always busy mowing the lawn or working on his car, and Mom was busy with my baby sister or doing yard work. No one had time for me.

I sat on my swing thinking, *boy, oh, boy, not another weekend. No matter what I do or say, it just doesn't change the way things are done around here. Dad's too busy. Mom's too busy. There's no one around to even give me a push on my swing.*

It was then that I saw a flicker of light coming from the attic window. I ran into the house and up the stairs to see who was there. It was Auntie Nellie! She was cleaning out a big, heavy trunk.

"Can I help? Everyone's too busy to play with me, and there's nothing I can do about it," I said angrily.

In her soft, kind voice she said, "Come over here and try on these goggles and boots that your grandpa wore when he flew his airplane."

So I put on the goggles and boots, and I have to say, I looked really funny. "Wait," Auntie Nellie exclaimed, "there's something missing!"

She reached deep into her pocket, and out came an amazing orange cape with the words "Super C" on the back. Auntie Nellie told me to try it on.

As I put it around my shoulders, I looked in the mirror. "I feel strong and very powerful," I announced, "like I could do anything!"

"Now you're Super Casey," Auntie Nellie said. "You have the power to take control of things around here."

"What does it mean to take control?" I asked.

"It means *you* can make changes if you really want to and really try hard."

"You mean I can get Dad to play catch with me and Mom to bake cookies?" I asked.

"Of course," Auntie Nellie replied, but it didn't seem possible to me.

"But how?" I asked. I had to know. "I'm only a kid."

Auntie Nellie in her confident voice said, "Remember, you're Super C. You're not helpless. Now take a few minutes to think of a way you can get your mom and dad to spend time with you. Just take control."

I looked in the mirror and saw Super C. Suddenly, I had a great idea. I had to do something that would get their attention. Since Mom and Dad were always making appointments with people, I decided I would try this, too.

In my room I made a poster with pictures of what I wanted Mom and Dad to do with me.

With the poster in my hands and the cape on my back, I ran outside and sang out to Mom and Dad:

"I am Super C!

Sign up now to be with me.

Pick two things that we will do.

Then write the time we'll start them, too!"

Dad picked reading stories and playing baseball, and Mom picked riding bikes and making cookies.

Auntie Nellie was right again! My Super C cape helped me understand that I could change the way things were done on the weekend. Mom and Dad told me they thought the poster was a very clever way to get their attention.

Now we talk about making plans for things we all want to do on the weekends. I keep my Super C cape under my bed, just in case I need to take control!

# PARENT/TEACHER NOTES
## Chapter 5: Feeling Ignored by Busy Parents

**Cue:** "Everyone's too busy to play with me, and there's nothing I can do about it."

**Problem/Stressor:** Casey is feeling somewhat helpless and unable to get his parents to actively engage with him. Because this has been occurring for several weekends in a row, he believes that there is nothing he can do to change the situation. In other words, Casey feels a disconnect between his attempts to get what he needs and the desired outcome. As a child, he believes he won't be able to get his dad to play catch with him or his mom to bake cookies. Over time, children will accept this feeling of learned helplessness and won't attempt to remedy the situation by altering their own behavior or taking control. As a consequence of repeatedly failing to accomplish his goal of getting his parents' attention, Casey may stop trying not only in this setting but in other social situations as well.

**Technique:** Auntie Nellie helps Casey by explaining that he can take control of the situation. Rather than giving up and playing by himself, Auntie Nellie shows him that even kids have resources they can use to take charge. As a result, they will feel good about initiating behaviors that work to change how others treat them. This feeling or perception of control will then spread to other social situations and promote feelings of competence and increased self-esteem.

**Other situations in which this technique may be useful:**

- Not being called on in class
- Not being chosen on a team
- Performing poorly on a test

# CHAPTER 6

# Another Way to Save the Day

Have you ever had strep throat? You know, your throat really hurts when you swallow? Well, I got it bad while Auntie Nellie was visiting. I even got red spots on my face! I remember I got sick the day my family and I were supposed to go to the circus.

The night before the circus, I dreamed about seeing the lions, tigers, and elephants, and eating cotton candy. I was so excited when I woke up that morning! I ran into the bathroom to get washed, and then I saw myself in the mirror.

"Mom! Mom! Come quick! Something is wrong with me. Hurry! Hurry!"

Mom came running upstairs and tried to calm me down after seeing the rash on my face and neck. "You must have gotten sick from your friend Lucas," she said. "I'm afraid you won't be able to go to the circus today."

"It's not fair!" I screamed. "It's just not fair! I want to go!"

Mom went downstairs to call the doctor. I was so angry that I threw all my stuffed animals down on the floor.

Just then Auntie Nellie walked in to find the mess in my room. As she looked around, Auntie Nellie laughed and said, "Why, it looks like a circus around here." With both hands she reached very deeply into one of her pockets and lifted out another amazing gadget—a giant bank with "Save-the-Day Idea Bank" written across it.

"Instead of saving coins in this bank," explained Auntie Nellie, "you save ideas that you can use when things aren't going the way you planned. If one idea doesn't work out, you try another one."

I looked around at all of my stuffed animals on the floor. I had an idea! I could make a circus right here in my room. All I needed were some boxes to make the cages for the animals and a large ring for the animal parade.

I found some boxes in the basement that I used for the animal cages. Then I used a rope to tie the cages together. I turned off the lights, pulled down the shade, and used my night light as a spotlight on the ring.

I was having so much fun that I forgot all about how angry I had been.

That's when Auntie Nellie told me that there would be other times in my life when I would be disappointed, because plans often change and promises are sometimes broken.

"Instead of getting angry, staying angry, and not having any fun," she said, "think of new ways to save the day."

I looked around my room and came up with lots of ideas to put in my new idea bank to use for some other time. I could always paint on my easel, play with my cars, or put on a puppet show. "There is more than one way to have a good time," I announced proudly.

"That's right," agreed Auntie Nellie. "Just remember, if one idea doesn't work, try something else from your bank."

"OK, Auntie Nellie," I said. "Now I'm going to save this day!"

Then I shouted, "Ladies and gentlemen, Casey's greatest show on earth will begin in five minutes. Don't be late!"

# PARENT/TEACHER NOTES
## Chapter 6: Handling a Major Disappointment

**Cue:** "It's not fair! It's just not fair! I want to go!"

**Problem/Stressor:** For a long time, Casey has been anticipating the fun of going to the circus. When he gets sick and can't go, Casey's response toward this stressor is to get angry and physically throw down all of his stuffed animals.

**Technique:** Auntie Nellie shows Casey that he can modify these kinds of stresses by taking direct action after reappraising or reinterpreting the situation. Specifically, Auntie Nellie helps Casey reappraise the stressful situation by introducing the "Save-the-Day Idea Bank." Instead of becoming angry and physically acting out, Auntie Nellie provides a means for Casey to store ideas that can be called upon whenever he meets stressful situations and disappointments in life.

Auntie Nellie challenges Casey to think of other activities that would also be fun and enjoyable. Casey sees firsthand that creating a circus with his own stuffed animals is an enjoyable substitute for going to the actual circus. In addition, in his own circus, he gets to be the ringleader. In this way, Casey learns a new coping method in which he replaces disappointing situations with opportunities to engage in activities that are just as much fun. You can encourage the child to be proactive and have ideas ready to be implemented. This coping skill will minimize the negative affect (i.e., anger) that often accompanies disappointment.

**Other situations in which this technique may be useful:**

- Friend cancels a play date
- Family plans change
- School program is cancelled

# CHAPTER 7

# MARY JAYNE'S PARTY

**W**henever I heard the words, "It's bedtime," I used to scream, "Just ten more minutes!" or "Let's read one more story!" or "I can't sleep!" This all changed on the last night of Auntie Nellie's visit. That night when I refused to go to bed, Auntie Nellie told me about Mary Jayne's party.

"To be invited to Mary Jayne's party," Auntie Nellie started, "you must be in your pajamas, have your hands and face washed, and your teeth brushed."

I loved going to parties, so I quickly washed up, put my pajamas on, and got into bed under the covers. I couldn't believe it when Auntie Nellie pulled a Glow-in-the-Dark Birthday Hat from her magical pockets!

As she put the Glow-in-the-Dark Birthday Hat on my head, she explained, "Now I want you to close your eyes and imagine all the sights, sounds, and smells I am about to describe. By thinking about what I'm going to tell you, we will be playing a game, but just with your mind. Your body will be all set to go to sleep."

Auntie Nellie continued in her soft voice. "Sometimes you might want to play other games with your mind, like thinking about going fishing with your dad or collecting seashells on the beach on a hot summer day. The most important thing to do in playing these games is to use your imagination. Do you think you can do that while I tell you about Mary Jayne's party?"

"I'll try," I said. I pulled my blanket up to my chin, closed my eyes, and listened to Auntie Nellie's soothing voice.

*"There were a lot of happy boys and girls at Mary Jayne's party, and they were all in their pajamas! Some kids were crunching on freshly popped popcorn coming out of a giant machine that looked like a dinosaur. In another corner, children were lined up in front of a man giving out cotton candy in three different colors—pink, purple, and blue. You could almost taste the cotton candy melting in your mouth. On the other side of the room, kids were playing balloon toss and pin-the-tail on the elephant."*

*"All of a sudden, the lights flickered and everyone knew to get in their seats. All the lights went out, and Mary Jayne's mother walked into the room holding a gigantic cake. You could only see the lights of the candles. Everyone started singing Happy Birthday to Mary Jayne. The time came for Mary Jayne to blow out the candles. Everyone counted 1—2—3, and with the biggest breath she could take in, Mary Jayne made a wish and blew out all of the candles."*

"What do you think she wished for, Casey?" asked Auntie Nellie. "What would you wish for?"

My Auntie Nellie told me that she would ask me for my answers in the morning. She gave me a kiss on my forehead, tucked me in, and put my Glow-in-the-Dark Birthday Hat on my dresser.

As she turned to leave my room, she said, "There may be other nights when you have trouble falling asleep, Casey. But just remember that you can do something about it!" Then Auntie Nellie began to sing:

**"It can be fun to be in bed,**

**If you play the game and use your head.**

**Close your eyes and pretend to see,**

**A wonderful place where you'd love to be."**

Auntie Nellie helped me again! All week she helped me during the day. Now she helped me to end the day, too. I turned over, hugged my white teddy bear, Snowy, and fell asleep thinking about birthdays, presents, wishes, and what I would tell my Auntie Nellie in the morning.

# PARENT/TEACHER NOTES
## Chapter 7: Trouble Falling Asleep

**Cue:** "Just ten more minutes!" "Let's read one more story!" and "I can't sleep!"

**Problem/Stressor:** Often times, bedtime is a stressor for both the child and parent. Children want to put off separating themselves from their parents and activities. Putting in place bedtime rituals will help ease children into the transition between awake time and sleep time.

**Technique:** Auntie Nellie teaches Casey how to use distracting imagery when he experiences trouble falling asleep. By attending to other stimuli, Auntie Nellie is able to direct Casey's attention away from the sometimes frustrating experience of falling asleep. Auntie Nellie makes Casey look forward to bedtime by having him imagine the pleasant sights, sounds, and smells of going to a birthday party. The requirement to attend this party is to be in pajamas and under the covers.

Auntie Nellie provides access to this technique in a rhyme, to help Casey retain the information:

> "It can be fun to be in bed,
>
> If you play the game and use your head.
>
> Close your eyes and pretend to see,
>
> A wonderful place where you'd love to be."

Verbalizing this poem with the child, and then getting the child to recite the poem before he goes to bed, will be a comforting way of ending the day and looking forward to bedtime.

**Other situations in which this technique may be useful:**

- Being in the dentist's chair
- Waiting in the doctor's office
- Sleeping away from home

# CHAPTER 8

# Using My Auntie Nellie's Gadgets

The week with Auntie Nellie went by so quickly. I was sad to say good-bye to her, but I was so happy she could help me! I won't forget how she helped me look at things differently and how she showed me that there were things I could do to make me feel better.

I found a special place in my room to put all of the gadgets that Auntie Nellie gave me: the Yes, I Can! Doll, Count-to-10-and-Try-Again Counter, Who-Can-I-Tell? Megaphone, Super C Cape, Save-the-Day Idea Bank, and my Glow-in-the-Dark Birthday Hat.

As I was thinking about Auntie Nellie, I looked out my window and saw Andy, my very best friend, who lives next door. She was sitting on her front step looking very sad.

I ran over to Andy's house and asked, "What's wrong, Andy?" Andy said, "I don't want to talk about it," and she ran off, almost crying.

"I don't want to talk about it" was something I used to say. I remembered using those very same words the day some kids in school called me names. I ran back to my house, got my Who-Can-I-Tell? Megaphone, and called out to Andy. "COME ON, ANDY. TELL ME WHAT HAPPENED. YOU'LL FEEL BETTER IF YOU DO. MAYBE I CAN HELP!"

Andy thought it over and slowly said, "I was supposed to sleep over at my Grandma's house tonight, but she just called and said she has to go away and cancel our plans."

"I know how it feels when somebody breaks a promise," I said. "But I bet you could sleep over at your Grandma's another night."

"I guess so," Andy admitted, feeling a little bit better. "But my day is still ruined. My sleeping bag is packed and now I have nowhere to go."

I thought about what Auntie Nellie had told me when I couldn't go to the circus the day I got sick. Suddenly, I remembered my Save-the-Day Idea Bank and Auntie Nellie telling me to think of ways to save the day.

"I'll be right back," I yelled and ran home to get my Save-the-Day Idea Bank. When I told Andy about it, I exclaimed, "I have a great idea. Why don't we pitch a tent in your backyard and pretend we're sleeping out in the woods?"

Andy got excited and said, "Yeah! Why don't you bring over your sleeping bag, flashlight, and canteen?"

Andy and I spent the rest of the day pretending that we were camping out in the woods. We took turns talking to each other through my Who-Can-I-Tell? Megaphone. We had so much fun! The gadgets from Auntie Nellie's magical pockets came to the rescue again—this time for my friend *and* me!

## THE END

# PARENT/TEACHER NOTES
## Chapter 8: Trying Out New Coping Skills

**Problem/Stressor:** In this chapter, Casey recognizes that his friend's reactions to stressful situations are similar to how he reacted before he learned the techniques from Aunt Nellie. Armed with a variety of new coping techniques, Casey is determined to help his friend, just as Auntie Nellie helped him.

**Technique:** This last chapter promotes the idea of giving children opportunities to *practice* their newly acquired coping skills in interpersonal situations. Casey recalls the cues that triggered his own stress response, and now he is able to show his friend how these stressors can be reappraised as challenges, not threats, and turned into positive situations. In this way, the coping skills are reinforced and shown to be effective. As is demonstrated in this last chapter, it is often easier for a child to pick up behaviors from a peer than for a child to understand or model the behavior of an adult.

*Author's Note: It is also important to recognize that not all children will call on these new coping skills as quickly as Casey. As with learning any new skill, giving the child ample opportunities to practice the new coping skills is essential. Developing confidence in using these coping skills when faced with stressful situations will help develop healthy habits for life.*

# About the Authors

**Monica H. Schaeffer, Ph.D.**, is a health psychologist who has conducted research and led workshops on stress and decision-making and stress management. She has been published in a number of professional journals on the effects of environmental stress, commuter stress, and illness severity. After studying stress in adults, both acute and chronic, Dr. Schaeffer recognized that children could benefit from possessing a repertoire of coping techniques to prevent the harmful effects of stress. In fact, the stories and techniques included in this book began taking shape when her oldest daughter communicated that she was not satisfied with simply having bedtime stories read to her and would exclaim, "tell me a story from your mind." Currently Dr. Schaeffer is the president of the non-profit VITAL, Inc. (www.vitalinc.org) and facilitates workshops on ethical wills/legacy letters. Her hobbies include photography, travel, and museum hopping.

**Shelley R. Baker** began working in and writing for the field of public relations and marketing after earning a B.S. degree in Public Communication from Boston University. She has extensive writing experience, including writing press releases, newsletters, articles, and stories. While navigating through the challenges of motherhood, Shelley was past president and served on the boards of directors of several community organizations. She most recently worked as the director of client and community relations for a certified public accounting firm. Shelley's experience with children comes from years of raising her own and spending extensive time helping to care for her eight grandchildren. That, as well as her writing and communication background, put her in a unique position to collaborate on this book.

# About the Illustrator

**Janie Secatore** is a graduate of the Massachusetts College of Art. She was a graphic designer and former marketing and communications director. Janie has also expressed her talent in murals, watercolors, hand-painted furniture, and other decorative arts. Illustrating *Auntie Nellie's Magical Pockets* is her first foray into children's book illustration. Janie found that creating visual images for both Casey and Auntie Nellie was a true joy.

23099835R00039

Made in the USA
Charleston, SC
12 October 2013